Elephant
Island

Antarctica

To
Krista

Donald Page

Dedication

I dedicate this story to **Sir Ernest Shackleton,** the Antarctic explorer who survived a most perilous two-year trek, from 1914 to 1916, in the sub-Antarctic regions of Elephant Island and beyond. Shackleton did this with courage and a unique leadership style which was most notable in my view and worthy of bedtime discussion. The story of Shackleton's experiences allows kids to move from courage and leadership demonstrated in fiction to a real life adventure of how one very strong leader brought an entire crew back safely from the unimaginable.

Shackleton's Way—"By Endurance We Conquer"

A Special Thanks

To First Lady **Laura Bush** for welcoming my first book, *The Feather-Dusted Easter,* into the White House for the annual Egg Roll Festival in 2001.

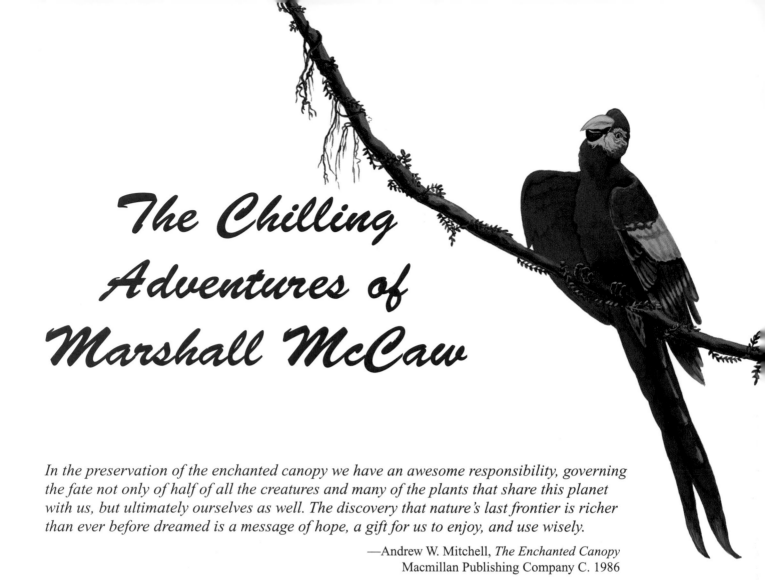

The Chilling Adventures of Marshall McCaw

In the preservation of the enchanted canopy we have an awesome responsibility, governing the fate not only of half of all the creatures and many of the plants that share this planet with us, but ultimately ourselves as well. The discovery that nature's last frontier is richer than ever before dreamed is a message of hope, a gift for us to enjoy, and use wisely.

—Andrew W. Mitchell, *The Enchanted Canopy*
Macmillan Publishing Company C. 1986

**A Story Written by
Charlet Faye**

**Illustrated by
Audrey S. Haddock**

**Cover Design and Illustrative Planning
By Charlet Faye
with Audrey S. Haddock**

FayeHouse Press International

Copyright © 2005, FayeHouse Press International
ISBN 0-9655222-1-0
LCCN 2003099719
All Rights reserved.

It was sundown in the rainforest and the Parrot Patrol was scanning the forest's edge. This was where the Bandit Bird had last laid its trail of destruction. The situation was more serious now than ever before. Martha Parrot had lost a baby. The outlaw bird had knocked it out of the nest and the nestling had died from the fall.

Marshall McCaw felt that all eyes in the forest were on him. He had to end this senseless destruction! He would bring the heartless bird to justice. But for Martha Parrot, what was justice? Marshall had to act, NOW!

Marshall talked with the grieving mother parrot and expressed his deep sadness for her loss. He vowed that a hunt would begin that very night. Marshall McCaw bowed like the parrot gentleman that he was and then was off. It was time to organize the hunt.

The Rainforest Community was lucky to have a wise and courageous bird like Marshall McCaw. He had made the forest a safer and more civilized place for all. Marshall began by informing his Patrol that it was time to start brainstorming. All ideas were welcomed and needed. He warned his Patrol that this would be a test of all their skills and courage.

Max, Marshall's best Patrol Bird, was the first to share a possible plan of attack.

It was thrown into the ring of Patrol Members, chewed
on, snipped at and squawked about! Other ideas
followed, and it was clear to Marshall why these were
the birds chosen to be here today. He perched tall on
the buttress root overlooking the group of dedicated
birds in what had become their place. Benches and
benches of buttress roots from the big, old rainforest
tree towered over the river, kept company by many
smaller fruit trees. This was their place,
Patrol Central.

Marshall felt proud of the Patrol. They
had learned to work well in the three years
that they had been together. The Patrol
had become a force of good
throughout the Forest Canopy.

The winds were whipping through the brightly colored plumes of the Patrol. Night would soon fall over the rainforest. Marshall McCaw instructed the members of the Patrol to scan their areas one last time; he himself would see that Martha Parrot was safe in her tree home.

After some last-minute chatter, the meeting began to break up.
But quite suddenly, from the corner of his eye Marshall noticed a
slight disturbance in the underbrush. Marshall winked and he and
the rest of the Parrot Patrol acted as if they were breaking up for
the night. He subtly gestured to his Patrol and, though they
acted like they all were heading for home, an attempt to
surround the secret onlooker began.

But the onlooker was ahead of the game and like a rocket SHOT from the underbrush!

Marshall grabbed the closest member of his Patrol. They darted after the rocket-like bird. Marshall shouted, "Keep your eyes open, Max! I don't want to lose him to nightfall!"

Max, struggling to keep up, to see, shouted, "I can't see him!"

Marshall's thoughts were racing. He and his lone partner were facing one of the most difficult chases of their careers in the Forest Canopy.

"It's no use. I'm no help! I can't see and I can't keep up!" Max squawked again.

Marshall shouted, "Go, go back! Alert the Patrol!"

"But Marshall, you need back up!" Max insisted.

"Go! That's an order!" Marshall commanded.

Max dropped his beak and dove out of the chase.

Marshall's thoughts were running one into another. He wondered if he was letting his anger cloud his thinking. But no, he could still see his target! This was right. He was Marshall! "Go, go!" he pushed himself angrily. On and on he flew into what had now become a haze. A chill came over him. He slowed his flight, looking, searching, but as the dusk had grown dark with violent storm clouds, he could no longer see. He had lost the mysterious onlooker! No! He had let his anger guide him. It was time to turn back, but what was back?

Marshall McCaw was lost. He was sure that the outlaw bird had doubled back, that he had tricked Marshall. Marshall hoped that the Parrot Patrol would not freeze up and let this mistake, his mistake, start a panic in the Forest Canopy.

He would glide now and try to save his energy. When morning broke he could get his bearings and find his way home. Like a bad dream, this too would have an ending. A cool breeze started to blow through his ruffled plumes. The big parrot had never been out of the forest. He shivered and glided on.

Common sense told Marshall to turn away from the cool air, but the winds were picking up, making the direction that he wanted harder and harder to keep. "Push! Push, McCaw!" He squawked loudly to himself. Soon the struggle became too great. The winds gave him no choice. "I must land. I've got to land!" Marshall moaned.

But there would be no landing for Marshall. The gale-force winds and now the torrential rain had him in their grips. In his mind he thought that this might be his last flight . . . shivering with cold, a prisoner of the storm . . . his fate was left to the wind.

Morning broke and found Marshall still in flight. The big parrot would soon perish if he could not get down.

The winds began to slow, giving Marshall more control over his flight. Looking down through the cloudy haze, he shook his head and looked again. Could it be that he was over water?

It was just a matter of time now and his struggle would be over. He could never survive the water that loomed below. This was a flight for his life. One more flap, another glide! Just a little more. If only he could see . . . JUST ONE MORE FLAP!

It was no use. Marshall was heading down, closer and closer to the water's surface. Marshall was a brave parrot. He would keep his beak held high. But no matter, soon he would be in the water.

But wait, what was this?! . . . CRASH! SLIDE! BRRRRRRRR! Marshal felt pain and freezing cold! It wasn't a splash, but a hard, chilling, painful crash-slide, and Marshall looked around . . . dazed and confused. He wasn't in the water. Marshall had hit a free-floating iceberg! What Marshall thought would be certain death turned out to be a chilling, painful surprise.

At least he wasn't in the water, Marshall thought, still surrounded by the
breezy haze that had been his nightmare from the start. He could no longer keep
his eyes open. The berg tossed and rolled. Marshall was in bad shape, but alive.
Soon, with the constant movement, he fell helplessly into a deep, deep sleep.
The berg floated on and on . . . through that night and into the next day.

"Excuse me, I hope you don't mind a bit of company," Pete Penguin said, staring curiously at his rather unusual berg companion. "My lunch was in a hurry today," Pete Penguin continued. "Say, are you okay?" Pete was tapping Marshall's brightly-feathered shoulder.

Marshall McCaw was on guard, but relieved to see that the new arrival was a friendly sort. He answered, "Well sir, I feel I've gotten a little too far from home. I don't know what you were doing for lunch, but I could use some directions to the nearest fruit tree."

"Well my friend," Pete responded, "I think you're quite lost. And about the fruit trees, you won't find any around this berg! Hey, can you fly?"

Marshall fluttered and flapped his wings and with a brief leap into the air, he answered Pete's question.

Pete appeared concerned and for the first time in the big parrot's life Marshall felt afraid. Marshall then broke the silence. "I'm Marshall McCaw. What's your name?"

"Pete Penguin's the name."

"You know, Pete, I thought I was doomed. Why, it's a miracle that I'm alive! Good grief . . . I'm sitting on an iceberg. I just can't believe . . ." Marshall began, when all of a sudden the berg started quaking and shaking, tossing and turning . . . Marshall was feeling frightened, but mostly confused, since it was a calm and sunny day.

Then from the ocean's surface popped a black, shimmering, bright, white, and, "Oh my! A mouth!" Marshall squawked in pure terror. The next few minutes seemed like a lifetime to Marshall McCaw.

There was a frightening pause and then ever so boldly Pete Penguin yelled out, "K. Whale, is that you?" The only response Pete got were two big glaring eyes peering down at him. He didn't know why they were peering . . . but they were definitely peering. "Uh . . . have you had your lunch today K. Whale?"

"Yup, Petie sure did." K. Whale answered slowly.

With a sigh of relief, Marshall McCaw looked on, shivering and wondering if he should try to fly again. What a strange situation Marshall found this to be. He hadn't eaten in days and his thoughts started to run. He wondered about home and if the Parrot Patrol had captured the Bandit Bird. He missed home, but he couldn't think about that now; he had to have food. He was feeling so very weak!

Finally, Pete indicated that Marshall could relax, giving the big parrot an "okay" sign. "K. Whale and I are friends!" Pete explained. Marshall tried, as he listened to the large creature ramble on about the giant wooden whales that scoured the ocean for krill. How dangerous they were! "It's a real jungle out there!" K. Whale bellowed.

Marshall cackled quietly, still feeling uncomfortable with the size of this latest marine discovery.

"Come on, K. Whale, we have a guest! And not a very comfortable one," Pete snorted.

"Yah, sorry, hello, ah, nice to meet you. Was it Marshall?" K. Whale asked.

"Yes, thank you K. Whale. I'm afraid I'll be needing some help. I'm a stranger in a strange land."

"You know, Marshall McCaw," Pete insisted, "after we land this berg you'll need to tell us where in the world you've come from!"

Marshall nodded with a tired smile and said, "That's easy, I've come from the tropical rainforest. But where in the world am I now?"

"Well my friend," Pete said, amazed, "as a matter of fact you happen to be south of the southern-most tip of South America! And in fact, Marshall, for your species, you are frightfully close to the South Pole. Antarctica!" Pete continued, "We'll have to be quick about getting you out of this ocean and into some winter gear. Those colorful feathers are nice but they'll never do the job here."

"Look out!" K. Whale shouted, and from his
blowhole spouted a fountain of krill . . . many of
which landed on the berg. "Eat. Come on,
they're good!"

Seeing that K. Whale had joined the struggle for Marshall's survival, Pete set out in the direction of Elephant Island so that he could contact the Penguin Hot Line. He made a connection several miles from the berg. The message read:

TO ALL ALBATROSS ON OR

NEAR ELEPHANT ISLAND:

EMERGENCY—PLEASE HELP!

NEED GRASSES DELIVERED.

TROPICAL BIRD IN TOW . . .

HEADED FOR ELEPHANT ISLAND,

AWAITING RETURN MESSAGE.

PETE PENGUIN

Pete remained in the area to make sure that the request would be received by the albatross. He floated, bobbed and played, and waited and waited.

Marshall McCaw, as wet as ever and much colder than before, started slurping down an unusual ocean meal that was, well, good, and very much alive. While Marshall clumsily chased his first meal in days, he began to thank K. Whale. Talking with a mouth full of krill, Marshall began, "You, sir, are a most kind and generous fish and I . . ."

"Oh, absolutely," interrupted K. Whale. "No problem. But you know, Marshall McCaw, I'm not a fish. Nope, I'm a mammal. I breathe air just like you and Petie do." And with that, K. Whale dove down and began nudging the berg toward Elephant Island, the Sub-Antarctic island that Pete called home.

Pete finally received the return message from the albatross. It had made it through to Albert Albatross and he agreed to the request. He and a large group of his friends had already begun the journey. Pete was pleased that Albert Albatross had responded so quickly . . . Pete could begin his journey back to the berg and his friends.

Looking up from the berg, Marshall observed a very large flock of birds off in the distance. They seemed to be heading in his direction. They were huge, gliding creatures that appeared frozen in the sky. As K. Whale rolled to the surface to gulp air, Marshall yelled out, "Hey look, K, look at those whales of the sky!"

K. Whale glanced up and before he dove back down he said, "Yah, albatross."

In the next few minutes, Marshall found that he was under an amazingly systematic grass rain, which was both timely and graceful. Marshall realized that this had to be the work of Pete, his penguin pal. Then as gracefully and quietly as the albatross had flown in, they were gone. They left behind towering mounds of dry, warm grasses. Things were much more comfortable for Marshall now. He swore that he would one day repay Pete Penguin and K. Whale for all of their trouble.

The berg was rocking. The ocean seemed to be dancing around him . . . for the first time since the accident, he felt safe and warm. It was a warmth that he had not felt since he left the forest. Pete seemed committed to seeing him through this, Marshall thought. He missed his new friend and hoped that he would return soon. K. Whale was still with Marshall, though he couldn't see him. He could feel the occasional nudge of the mammal's large snout whenever the berg was pulled off course by the strong currents.

Marshall trembled and tried not to think of the impossible task of getting back home. With a stomach full of krill and warm, grassy wishes from the albatross, he soon fell into a peaceful sleep.

The waves came up and rolled back down. The breeze was calm. The sounds were few, but constant. Every now and then the huge mammal would roll up for air and then disappear again below the surface to a task that he chose to do because he cared.

Around sundown Marshall awoke groggily. It had been a
much needed sleep. He peeked out from his warm nest, disappointed that Pete
had not yet returned. A little more browsing around led him to a very neatly
piled dinner of krill. That K. Whale! He was something. He possessed an
attitude that Marshall wished to share with the Forest Community when he
returned . . . if he returned. He wanted to be back there right now, this very
minute. He sighed and thought that certainly he would not be getting back the
same way he had arrived! His Patrol would never believe this story. Marshall was
sure that they would all think this a very imaginative bump on the head.
    Marshall was deep in thought when Pete popped onto the berg . . . "Hey!"
Pete crowed proudly. "You look uh, good Marshall McCaw, and warm!" The
albatross had more than filled the order and Pete himself was amazed at the
speed that his huge bird friends had displayed.
    Marshall didn't mind the crowing. He too was very proud of the clear
thinking that this water bird had exercised. "I could use a bird like you in my
Forest Patrol," Marshall said admiringly.
    "Well thank you very much, Marshall, but it's for certain that my flights
will never be through the forest trees. But if I were a bird with higher thoughts,
then we'd be in business!" Marshall and Pete peeped and squawked and enjoyed
the light mood.
    "You know Pete, this has been hard for me. This Antarctic breeze is a
killer! I can't help but wonder how in the world I'm ever going to get back
home."
    "Look," Pete reassured, "let me worry about that."
    "I'm really going to miss you, Pete."
    "Yeah, me too . . . now look at that pile of krill," Pete said, amazed. "That
K. Whale, he's all heart." Marshall cackled, pretty loudly this time. "To have a
friend with a heart the size of a whale!"
    "How lucky we are that K. Whale is as good as he is big," agreed Marshall.
The two friends quietly and contentedly finished their dinner. Soon, with the
rhythmic rocking of the berg, Marshall was lulled to sleep—warm, content,
and safe.

After resting a bit, Pete dove into the water to spend some time with K. Whale. Down and down he went to the depths of the berg. He found his friend faithfully nudging the huge piece of ice. Pete clowned around, joining K. Whale and pretending that he too could help. K. Whale found this very funny and let out a big whale chuckle, sending a massive air bubble rising up toward the surface.

As Pete watched the bubble float up through the water, he caught sight of a motionless body floating near the surface. Like lightning, he charged toward what appeared to be Marshall. K looked and he knew, he knew it was Marshall and with pain in his heart he shot to the surface and blew out all the water he could from his blowhole. He then dove to scoop the unconscious parrot into his whale-sized mouth, allowing the bird to tumble gently into his warm, cavernous body. He then rose to join Pete near the berg.

Pete quickly slid onto the berg as K. Whale floated up, "Did you get him?" Pete asked, a tear rolling down his cheek.

The big whale's eyes were filled with disappointment as he nodded yes.

"Let me in, K! He's our friend, we can't let him go now!"

"Go. Hurry Petie, I'll float. I'll be very still."

So Pete, putting his complete faith in the whale, started down into the live, moist, and very warm shelter. Pete was worried as he entered K. Whale's body. How long had Marshall been in the water? He just had to be okay.

As he worked his way through, Pete thought that this was really a very good environment for Marshall, if only he could find him safe . . .

And then from the depths Pete heard a dull echoing, Cough-cough, spurt, wheeze!

He waddled closer and closer to the sounds . . . Pete's eyes lit up with excitement as he spotted his new friend. Far off in a corner, in a puddle of water, was an alive and fluttering Marshall McCaw.

Marshall was upset and shouted, "Pete! Did he eat you too?" as he sputtered and spurted water from his beak.

"Oh Marshall, you're okay. You haven't been eaten, K. Whale rescued you. You were knocked off the berg by a wave. The waters around Cape Horn can be very dangerous; I should never have left you," Pete replied with great sorrow. "You've been dazed by the icy waters. You need to rest now. K has agreed to be your floating house. He's waiting to hear that you're okay.

Marshall sat shivering. He knew that Pete was right. "Okay," he agreed. "I'll be fine."

"Don't worry," Pete said reassuringly, "I'll see you when I get back. I have to swim out and send another message on the hot line. I've made a decision, if the albatross are willing . . ."

Marshall listened carefully. He trusted Pete but still he said, "It sounds hopeful and I thank you for all of your trouble, but I really don't know what the albatross will be able to do, Pete."

"I really can't say now, Marshall, but I have an idea. I'll have to set up a meeting with Albert Albatross. He was the bird who organized the grass drop. He surely will be the one to help us now if anyone can."

As Pete waddled away he was mumbling to himself, "They'll have to think about the chicks at this time of year . . ." And then his thoughts ran to the interesting cloth house that the scientists had left on Elephant Island. Pete knew it was a special house because it had protected the scientists from the icy winds and rain. The humans were so fragile. If this could work for them, he believed that it could work for Marshall too.

Albert Albatross was a large, stately bird. He received the message as he stood on the rocky shoreline of Elephant Island.

Pete asked that Albert join them on the berg for a meeting, as the original plan was falling through and they would have to request the help of the albatross once again if their tropical friend was to survive.

Albert strutted over to discuss the new request that he had received on the hot line. He talked with some of the other males near the shore; and they were also joined by Agnes Albatross, the bird most often chosen to represent the ideas and interests of the female population on the island. Agnes agreed that it was most important and necessary for the albatross to help. All the females would need, in the absence of many of the males, would be a small team to help protect the new families from the dangers on the island.

There was a quick vote taken and it was decided, Albert would take two birds with him to the meeting on the berg. They loaded up with grasses again and in a short time were headed out toward the berg.

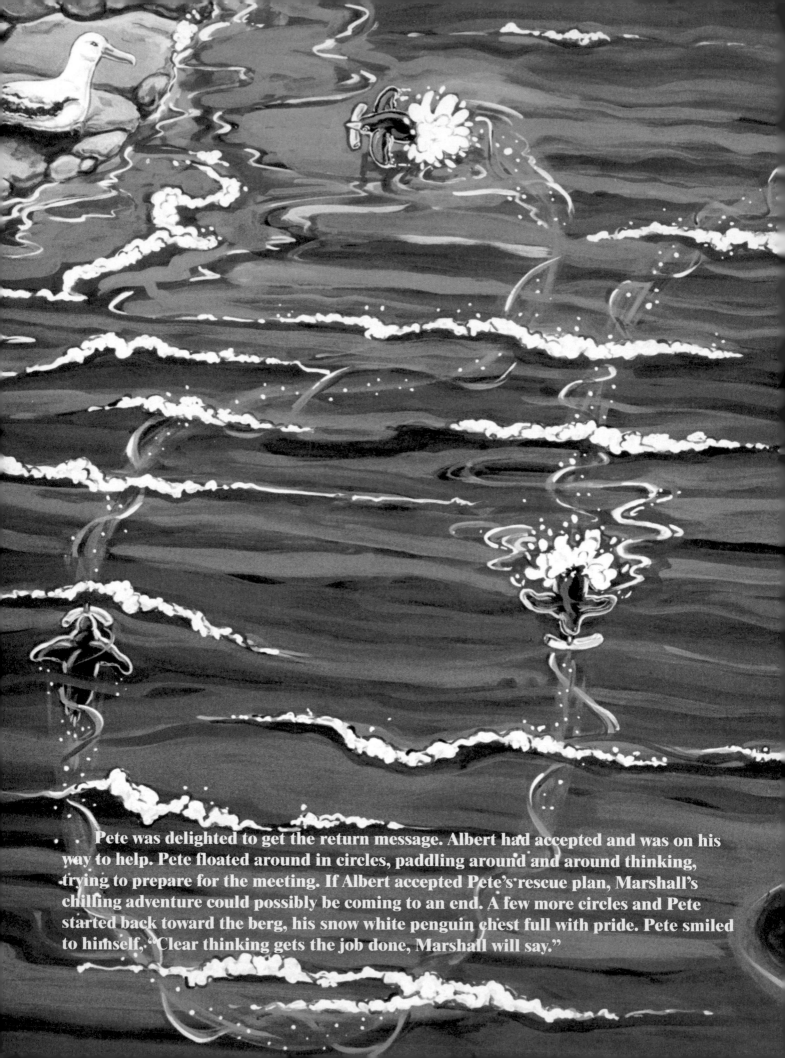

Pete was delighted to get the return message. Albert had accepted and was on his way to help. Pete floated around in circles, paddling around and around thinking, trying to prepare for the meeting. If Albert accepted Pete's rescue plan, Marshall's chilling adventure could possibly be coming to an end. A few more circles and Pete started back toward the berg, his snow white penguin chest full with pride. Pete smiled to himself, "Clear thinking gets the job done, Marshall will say."

As Pete approached the iceberg, K. Whale
flapped his tail in a funny kind of hello. Pete was
glad to see that K. Whale still had a sense of humor,
even though he had already missed a couple of meals.
"Any luck, Petie?" K. Whale asked curiously.
Pete slipped onto the berg, nodding positively. "They're
coming. Hey K, glad to see you're in a good mood."

From the south, three albatross were approaching. K. Whale let Pete in to check on Marshall, whom he found asleep in the warm tropical climate of K. Whale's body. As Pete came back out, the albatross were just about to land. One, two, three, each bird landed strongly, one right after the other.

Pete and K greeted the albatross warmly and then got on with the pressing business at hand. Albert said they must get on with the meeting, as he was concerned about the young birds back on the island and the many eggs that would be hatching at any time.

Pete began by talking about the special cloth house on the east side of the island, of the special qualities that he knew it possessed. Albert listened intensely, while the other birds appeared to be more curious about their leader's feelings in the matter.

Pete went on to say that he believed that this cloth house could be used to help get Marshall home. Albert looked on questioningly as Pete continued, "It's light weight and weather resistant and I believe it would be possible to get Marshall over the water safely, if we used it as a carrier. Once Marshall gets close to home, he can take off from the carrier and fly himself home."

Albert nodded and looked toward his fellow albatross. They seemed to agree that this was a reasonable plan. With their twelve-foot wingspan and strong flying capability, they felt that they could handle the task even with the extra weight.

The meeting went on and it was decided, Marshall would go home. Albert would be in charge of organizing the journey and he would let Pete know when they were ready. Pete Penguin thanked Albert and his friends for caring enough to help Marshall. Pete would miss his new friend. He knew K. Whale had grown fond of Marshall too. Maybe another time in a warmer place they would meet again.

The albatross were off to gather the needed items and organize their rescue mission. Pete and K. Whale breathed a sigh of relief and K said quietly, "You know Pete, it seems hard to imagine that we found a way home for our friend."

"I know," Pete agreed. "I better go and tell Marshall."

And with that, K. Whale stretched open his mouth and Pete made his way down with the good news. "Marshall!" Pete called. "Marshall McCaw!" Pete squawked more loudly now. Pete spun around in his stiff penguin style looking frantically for his friend. He couldn't see him anywhere. "Marshall!!"

"Hey Pete!" Marshall yelled down from high atop a rib bone. "Stop that spinning, you're making me seasick! Look at me, Pete. The wing is as good as new," Marshall boasted as he glided down toward a very surprised Pete Penguin.

"Bravo, Marshall! So you are strong enough to make the trip."

"Trip?" Marshall questioned with piqued interest, fluttering and flapping all around within his living home.

Pete excitedly informed Marshall that the albatross had agreed to give him a one-way air trip back to the forest. "You'll have to take off from the carrier you'll be riding on. Do you think you're strong enough?"

"I'm ready whenever they are," Marshall answered with a note of sadness.

Pete nodded and, as he made his way back out to the berg, told Marshall that he would be back down in a short while with the extra grasses that Albert had brought.

Marshall, deciding that he too could use the warmth of the sun on his back, also made his way up. "K. Whale, open please, it's me, Marshall. Remember me?"

K. Whale gently opened his mouth and Marshall zoomed out, flying high above the berg, over K. He was gliding around and around and then swooping down over Pete.

K. Whale followed the surprising activity with his big whale eyes. "Marshall! You're as good as new."

This was a happy parrot. "Hip-hip hurray for Marshall McCaw. Hip-hip hurray!" Pete and K. Whale cheered. Marshall landed proudly on the berg, this time with ease and dignity. K. Whale, amazed at the change in Marshall since he had fished him out of the icy waters, smiled the biggest smile that you could ever imagine.

"K. Whale, it's way past lunch. I'll be fine. You look like you could use a swim!" Marshall nestled amidst the grasses.

K. Whale gently left the berg and when he was far out he did a most spectacular whale jump! Pete and Marshall could hear him bellowing, "Hip-hip hurray, it's a good day!" And with a wave of his giant tail he disappeared below the glistening ocean surface.

Marshall sat warming in the sun while Pete dove into the water for a relaxing swim around the berg. Down and down he swam looking for an ocean snack for himself and Marshall.

A stillness fell over the berg; Marshall was alone now. He would have much to share with his Patrol and his forest friends. He could tell them about the bird who flies through water and of the gentle giant from the deep. He could tell about the lessons of survival that he had learned and those of special caring. Marshall was feeling very tired, as this day had been one of the most active of his stay on the berg. It was the day he had learned of his trip home.

The next thing Marshall realized was Pete shaking him, saying, "Wake up, Marshall! You should be plenty rested up for your trip today. The albatross will be here any time now with the carrier."

Word had spread far and wide of Marshall's presence on the berg. Creatures were starting to gather to say goodbye. Penguins were popping up everywhere around the berg, extending well wishes to Marshall for a safe passage back to his warm home.

And then there was K. Whale, his big body bobbing close by, tears welling in his eyes.

Marshall was moved by this show of support and felt a need to speak. He stood and began to talk about the courage and clear thinking of a wonderful penguin named Pete and of the tremendous sacrifices and patience of a very large mammal named K. Whale, whom he had the good fortune to get to know. He talked of how grateful he was to be alive on this day. He would never forget these days on the berg, days that he thought were his last. Now he found himself very much alive with a new feeling about the value of life and friendship.

As he spoke, the albatross
appeared on the horizon. It was quite
an interesting sight. From a distance the
creatures and carrier appeared to be a large
flying machine.

A silence fell over the group as the ten huge
albatross positioned themselves to land on the berg. Then
with continued calm they touched down, two by two, sure
and powerful.

Albert, serious and precise, informed
Pete that the farewell should be short; to
ensure the parrot's safety they would have to move
while the weather was good. This would be a long,
strenuous flight for the big birds.

In the very short time that he had, Pete tried to express how
much Marshall's friendship had come to mean to him. But the words
were hard to find. So he reached out with a gift that the group had gathered
for Marshall, krill wrapped in moist seaweed.

Albert was heaping grasses on the carrier and motioning for Marshall . . . It
was time now, time for Marshall to go home. It was time for friends to part and
life to go on as usual.

Marshall approached the carrier and situated himself, he looked at
K. Whale and K gave him a happy wink. Happy except for a large tear that
splashed down onto the berg. Marshall remembered back to the first time
he met K. Whale. To see this huge mammal slide out of the water, how
frightening he was. But how different he seemed now,
how very different.

And then, without warning, Albert's huge wings
began to flap, along with his flying partner's and
systematically, two by two they rose up like
stair steps above the glistening
morning water . . .

The next few minutes brought such an incredible sight that the group of marine animals forgot the sadness of the moment. They bobbed and tossed in the water, looking on in sheer amazement as Albert and his team of Wandering Albatross took off for the north with their valuable cargo.

All ten birds were up as the carrier slid off of the berg, swinging briefly just a few feet above the water's surface. Slowly the carrier rose up toward the sky, heading for the place that Marshall called home.

Marshall glided safely back into the rainforest and arrived home to his Patrol and his forest friends. He learned that the Bandit Bird had not been as lucky as he; the bird had perished in the storm. In an all out search for Marshall, Max had discovered the Bandit Bird. He was identified by some trinkets that were found near the body, trinkets that had been taken from Martha Parrot's tree home just days before.

In the Forest Canopy there were losses and lessons learned. And life goes on, peaceful once again with Marshall, Max, and the Patrol Birds ready and waiting for the next adventure to arise within their home in the Forest Canopy.

The End

TEACHERS AND PROFESSIONALS TALK

"*The Chilling Adventures of Marshall McCaw* is a refreshing story for children and adolescents. The challenges of the brilliantly colorful characters are much like those which Ernest Shackleton and his team boldly and courageously endured.

"The author eloquently combines fact with fiction to create a heartwarming story of courage, endurance, and the importance of friendship in our world today!"

—Cynthia M. Radovic BA, MA, BSN, CSP
   Children's National Medical Center
   Adolescent and Child Psychiatry
   Washington, D.C.

"Every loving parent wants more for their kids than they do for themselves, and every loving parent wants their kids to have an exalted life. This book will help to do that. Read it, and read it again!"

—Mark Victor Hansen
   Co-Creator of the *Chicken Soup for the Soul* series,
   New York Times Best Seller List

"Charlet Faye has created an adventure that will both challenge and intrigue the young reader. It encourages both creativity of thought and a sense of exploration. Young readers will hear a voice of hope through Marshall McCaw as he journeys into an unfamiliar environment, and achieves ultimate victory over fear with the help of unlikely friends."

—Yvonne Meyer
   Second Grade Teacher
   Windsor Farm Elementary School
   Annapolis, MD
   B. S. Education

"*The Chilling Adventures of Marshall McCaw* demonstrates the value of cooperation, creative problem solving, and above all, friendship. Charlet Faye's vividly illustrated tale of the animals native to the South American region merits a place on a child's bookshelf."

—Randall Rice M.Ed
   Principal
   Windsor Farm Elementary School
   Annapolis, MD

"What an example for the children of today! With wonderful words and feelings this book comes alive. From rain forests to penguins, Marshall McCaw will definitely have a place on my bookshelf. It will be a great addition to my curriculum for teaching about friendship, courage, the environment, and animal habitats. Thanks for a new look at an old story."

—Adrienne Evans
   Title I Reading Specialist, Literature teacher
   Westhaven Elementary School
   Belleville, IL

"Charlet Faye welcomes children to her family of beautiful birds through this wonderful tale. *The Chilling Adventures of Marshall McCaw* is an exciting story for readers of all ages that allows them to explore friendship, teamwork, and problem solving skills. From the rich and colorful illustrations of the Rainforest to the icy waters of Antarctica, I am sure that *The Chilling Adventures of Marshall McCaw* will capture and warm your heart as it has mine. I look forward to the next tale of Marshall McCaw and friends as they continue to explore new lands!"

—Grayce Simmons
   Retired teacher, volunteer
   Howard County Center of African American Culture, Inc.
   B. S. Education and Special Needs

South America